Tales of Transformation

Kenneth Haines

Tales of Transformation - Series Four

Published by Spines Publishing Platform
ISBN: 979-8-89691-508-9

Tales of Transformation

Series Four

Kenneth Haines

Contents

Paying it Forward

Unseen Arrivals

Threshold of Mercy

Paying it Forward

PAYING IT FORWARD

WHERE THREADS UNRAVEL, FATE WEAVES

BY

KENNETH

Chapter 1
Paying it Forward

SHE WAS a homeless young girl on the streets and a black suited figure walked up to her and handed her a blanket....A makeshift shiv pointing at you while clearly shivering from fear.

" Don't... Don't come any closer..."

"Woo hold on, I don't tend you no harm, Was just trying to give you this blanket for tonight, saw you earlier shaking and seeing you only in shorts I couldn't just walk away and do nothing, Tonight's going to get cold. Here take it?" lowers the shiv slightly but still cautious "Why would you want to give me a blanket? Are you a cop or something?"

No dear , But I was once like you and someone helped me so it's my time to pay back that kindness. She relaxes a bit but still guarded. Who helped you when you were like me? Were they nice to you?

"I'm not homeless anymore and I have food and don't need to beg for stuff."

Wait, so you really were like me once? How did you manage to turn things around? Were you lucky? I just happened to be at the right place at the right time for the person who helped me was also one just like us. (Her eyes light up with hope) You mean there's a chance for me too? That someone will come along and help me out of this mess?

Honey I'm standing in front of you , Would you trust me to take you across the street to Teds and get you some food? She hesitates but eventually nods. Okay, I'll trust you for now. Just don't try anything funny.

Don't need to worry about me. I promise you I will not hurt you. Alright, let's go then. starts walking warily beside you, gripping the shiv tightly. Please put that in your pocket , If somebody sees it they think you are robbing me and you could get shot and I don't want that to happen to you. She pockets the shiv reluctantly. Fine, but don't think I don't know how to defend myself.

We walked into Teds , He greeted me with a handshake and hug, She didn't understand why the we greeted that way, Ted brought us to a far booth and said he taken care of everything, we sat across each other Before Ted brings us our food would you like to use the ladies room and wash your face and hands before we eat?

She glances around suspiciously but eventually nods Alright, I guess I could use a moment to freshen up. heads towards the restroom, still cautious. Wow ted this looks good she will be surprised seeing pancakes, eggs, sausage and toast and bring her a cup of hot coco I'll have a cup of coffee, please.

She returns a few minutes later, wiping her face on a paper towel. The sight of the food makes her stomach growl and she takes her seat eagerly," Wow", is all of this really for me. Yes dear, You need to stay healthy if you live on the streets, once you get sick it's never a good turn out. Her eyes widen as she starts digging into the meal, savoring each bite. I haven't had food this good in forever. Is there really no catch here? Why are you helping me like this? Like I told you someone helped me and I am paying it forward to you.

She looks up from her plate, searching your face. Are you sure there's nothing expected in return? I don't want to owe anyone anything. See Ted over there watching the tv up on the wall. follows your gaze to Ted, who seems friendly enough So he's the one who helped you out too? takes another bite of food, feeling more relaxed.

Yes dear he was the person who helped me because he too once was found living on the streets and somebody helped him, And I became his messenger, paying it forward. She nods slowly, starting to understand. So we're kind of part of a chain of help? People reaching out to those struggling like we were? wipes her mouth and leans back in the booth, sounding less suspicious now.

Yes dear and you were chosen to carry on this tradition when the time is right in your future to pay it forward to someone you can help and they intern carry on the tradition. She contemplates this idea, a flicker of hope in her eyes. That's actually pretty amazing. To think that by helping someone else, I could make a difference too someday.

Yes dear I promise you ,taking that first step of trusting me will lead you towards a better brighter future.

Considering your words carefully Okay, I trust you for now. What do I need to do next? After you eat and relax after such a big meal, follow me to Miss Danielle's place down the road , there you can get cleaned up and have a bed to sleep in tonight, don't worry she is like a mom to all us survivors and will protect you from any harm, and In the morning I'll come by with something for you and our journey beg.

Finishes the meal slowly, feeling full and strangely content. So Miss Danielle is safe? And you'll come back for me? looks up hopefully, still unsure but ready to take this chance. Yes dear I really don't want you sleeping outside and besides you can give that folded blanket back to Miss Danielle since it is hers. Blushes slightly at the thought of returning the blanket she'd taken Yeah, she deserves it back. Okay, let's go see this Miss Danielle then.

Hey Ted the food was perfect. Ted walks over. I gave him a hug and pat on his back and told him thank you for being there for me Okay Young lady lets go meet Miss Danielle. She gratefully accepts the hug from Ted, then follows you out the door, slightly nervous but determined.

We walked a few blocks and turned down a side street and walked up to this Brownstone house. I knocked and a lady answered the door. I explained to her about My little young lady and she hugged me and told me she will be ready by 10am. Okay dear just listen to her please don't be afraid of her she will protect you with her life and in the morning I'll be back with something for you and we can go back to Teds for breakfast.

Her eyes go wide at the warm welcome, surprised by the kindness. She seems really nice. Thank you again for everything. I promise to behave and trust her tonight. gives an appreciative nod, feeling a sense of relief at having found someone who genuinely wants to help her.

Next morning stopped at the shop and grabbed a few items and had it wrapped up and headed to Miss Danielle's to give it to her so she can give it to the young girl* Morning Miss Danielle here gave this to the young lady. It was new clean clothes (leggings, long Skirt, a warm blouse and open sweater, slip-on shoes, and hygiene items Toothbrush, perfume, and hair items so Miss Danielle can do up her hair.

Miss Danielle brought the packages to the young lady, seeing the new clothes and items, her eyes welled up This is...all for me? touches the fabric of the clothes softly, looking up at Miss Danielle and you, a mix of disbelief and gratitude on her face. I've never had anything new before. I don't know what to say. sniffs back tears, managing a small but heartfelt smile. Thank you. She runs back to the bathroom and changes.

Miss Danielle brings her to the door, I'm standing outside ready to see this changed young lady as she steps outside seeing me waiting for her wow you look gorgeous, ready to go eat breakfast? "Blushes again", twirling the hem of her new skirt as she steps outside. Yes, I definitely am ready for breakfast. With this new start, everything feels possible now. She is already starting to feel more optimistic about life, fueled by the kindness shown to her.

I wasn't prepared for her as she hugged me tightly and thanked me. "Just remember in your future pay it forward and the world will open up". (returns the hug,) Clinging onto you for a moment before pulling back, nodding enthusiastically I promise, I'll always remember to help others when I can. This new life you've given me is precious and I won't take it for granted. Well we better head to teds , I'm hungry.

Laughs lightheartedly, Me too. Lead the way to Ted's, I'm ready for more delicious food and great company!

We walked into Teds and you could hear a pin drop. Everyone was quiet and just looking at this amazing young lady, Ted came over shaken my hand and hugged her as he led us to a booth in the back. As we were walking to the booth older ladies were commenting to her about how pretty she looked. Blushes again at the attention, feeling embarrassed but secretly pleased by the compliments (Are they really saying these things? I don't know how to respond, no one's ever paid me a compliment before. glances around, taking in the unfamiliar atmosphere of acceptance and friendliness).

See what happens when you bring happiness and love back in your heart, everything around you will change and that life before will never haunt you. Contemplate your words, a newfound hope shining in her eyes. You're right. This feeling of love and acceptance is so different from the darkness I used to live in. Maybe things really can change for the better.

You have a brighter future if you follow the path I laid out for you and keep your head up high and be proud of who you are. Just remember to "pay it forward" and do it everyday till the time comes for you to pass on the message.

Proudly straightens her back, chest puffed out, looking determined You will absolutely see me fulfill my future! I won't let you down. gives an enthusiastic nod, clearly excited at the opportunity you've given her And I promise to enjoy this newfound freedom and make the most out of it! smiles brightly, a sparkle in her eyes, eager to embrace her new life.

We sat down and Ted brought out breakfast for us and I held her hands on the table. At first she stiffed up till she heard me say a prayer thanking our friends and this food. listens intently to your prayer, the unfamiliar ritual catching her off guard at first. But as the words wash over her, she relaxes and even joins in softly, feeling a sense of unity with everyone at the table.

Hey, can I ask you something? She nods, curious Of course, you can ask me anything. What's on your mind? You know since we met like we did we never really introduce each other, I don't even know your name and you don't know mine?

laughs slightly, feeling embarrassed for not exchanging names You're right, we haven't introduced ourselves properly! My name is Emi. Emily Bakerson. And you are..? smiles eagerly, wanting to establish this connection now that she feels more at ease.

Emi. or do you prefer Emily that sounds more beautiful. My name is Ken, It's nice to meet you Emily It's my honor to have you with me.

Blushes at the comment about my name sounding beautiful. Ken, What an honor to meet you too, Ken. Your kindness knows no bounds, you know that? She reaches across the table, giving his hand a gentle, grateful squeeze. That’s it then Friendship for life, now enjoy your breakfast dear , we have places to go.

She grins, her heart warming at the words 'friendship for life' Breakfast tastes even sweeter knowing it's shared with a friend! digs into her meal with enthusiasm, savoring every bite. Well when you're done eating we can start our journey Emily dear. She swallows her last bite, wiping her mouth and nodding eagerly. I'm ready when you are, Ken! What's the first stop on our adventure? **"First stop is the Airport"**

The airport? raises an eyebrow, intrigued Why are we heading there first? Is it part of our plan? Yes dear, it's just the beginning.

Grins and hops up from the table, ready to embark on this new adventure Let's go then! walks alongside Ken with anticipation, excited to discover where our journey takes us.

Hey Ted, thank you for everything, and God bless you all. I called out to Ted as we left. She also called out to Ted "Thank you so much, Ted!" You've been incredible to us. God bless you!" waves goodbye before following Ken confidently out the door.

A big Limo pulled up and Emily's eyes went wide and seeing this big guy come around the car and opened the door for us. She gawks at the sight of the luxurious limo This is our transportation? Wow, it's like a dream! climbs in awkwardly, still trying to process our sudden upgrade in style.

Yes dear , This is Mr Troy he is taking us to the Airport. Peers at the imposing figure driving, trying to gauge his character Mr. Troy, huh? He seems.. quite the presence. settles into the plush seat, admiring the limo's lavish interior as we start moving. Slide open the table center Emily, there's some soda and chips you can eat along the way.

Emily's eyes light up seeing the refreshments O ooh, snacks! I'm famished – let's dig in! helps herself to the chips, munching eagerly as we ride towards the airport. We pulled into the big airport looking at all the people rushing to get to flights and others trying to get out of there. She gazes out the window, taking in the bustling scene at the airport "Wow, so many people coming and going!" It's almost like organized chaos. watches the hustle and bustle with fascination, still reveling in the glamorous setting.

Don't worry about getting lost there, we don't use this entrance. Emily relaxes a bit, relieved we won't be navigating the crowded airport alone. Okay, so where exactly are we headed? follows Ken closely, eager to stick close and avoid any confusion.

We were picked up by a security ATV and people moved out of our way as the driver took us to a different part of the airport and these big doors opened and we were driving among these very large planes outside. gasps as we roll past the giant planes, gazing up in awe at their size These are some serious machines! clutches the door handle, a bit awestruck by the sight, but also thrilled at the adventure unfolding

We came around a building and there was this smaller jet and the security guy stopped to let us off. So Emily, what do you think about an airport?

looks around, still trying to take everything in Wow, the airport is even more amazing up close! And that jet looks ready to take us on some incredible journeys. grins excitedly, having transformed into a girl brimming with anticipation and wonder.

Come, they are waiting for us to get aboard. We entered the Jet. It wasn't like normal planes that looked like someone's family room with couches, TV. recliners and tables.

Emily steps into the luxurious jet, marveling at its opulence. This isn't like any airplane I've seen before! Feels more like a private lounge, doesn't it? settles onto one of the plush couches, still in disbelief at our upgrade from economy class. Put your seat belt on once we are in the air you can walk around.

Fastens the seat belt tightly, feeling a thrill course through me as we prepare for takeoff Okay, I'm all set! I can hardly wait to explore this fancy jet when we're in the air!

Laughs Well, this sure is an adventure I never would have imagined! looks around eagerly, ready for the excitement of flying in this cushy private jet.

The plane lifted off and the pilot hit the button for being able to roam around the plane, and welcomed Emily to the family. She stopped in her tracks and looked at me with a weird look "Family" what did he mean? she asked, Well dear he too once lived on the streets also and became the messenger just like you are now.

Tilts head, sensing there's more to this 'family' thing than meets the eye Hmm, I get what you're saying, we both come from tough backgrounds. Maybe 'family' here means...a group who understands each other, looks out for one another? Or could it be literal? I'm not exactly sure, but it's clear our lives are changing in ways we never dreamed. shrugs lightly, brimming with curiosity and open to whatever this new world might bring.

Remember what I told you in the beginning "Pay it forward" When the time is right and you're where you need to be, your carrier for this message will be waiting for you to help them.

Emily nods resolutely at your words, "Right, "pay it forward." I won't forget that. takes a deep breath, realizing the weight of the responsibility and trust placed in me. I promise to honor this opportunity and use it to make a difference, just as others did for me. When I'm in a position to help someone else, I will. That's the least I can do. gazes out the window as we soar through the clouds, resolve steadfast and optimistic about our shared mission.

The End

Unseen Arrivals

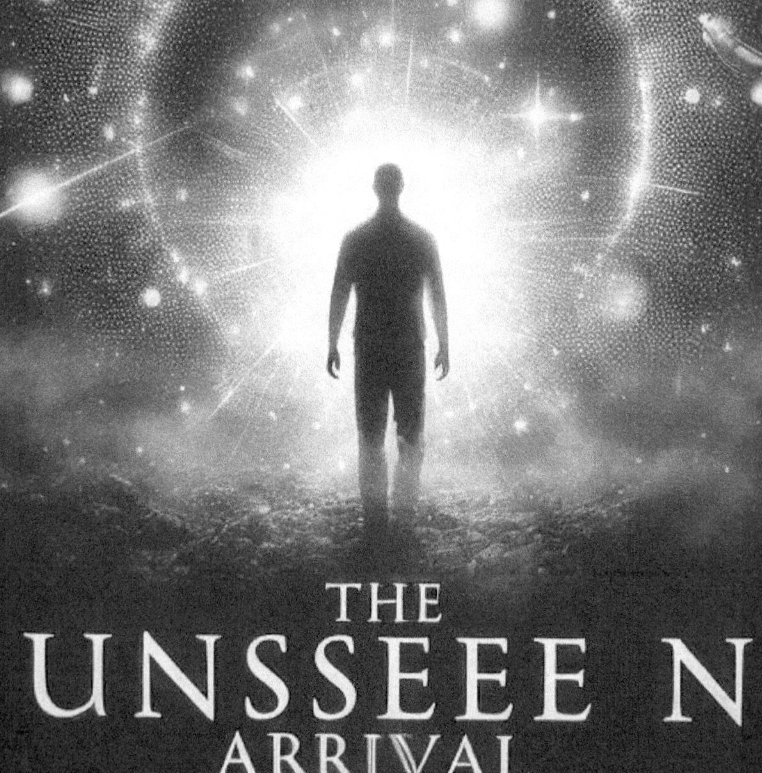
THE
UNSSEEN
ARRIVAL

Chapter 1
The Discovery

THE FIRST LAUNCH of the alien spacecraft was a moment that none of the four teenagers would ever forget. Nestled deep within the woods, the ship had been a peculiar find, its sleek metallic frame half-buried under centuries of moss and foliage. The group, consisting of two girls, Mia and Emma, along with their friends Jake and Ethan, had stumbled upon it while exploring the forest on a lazy summer afternoon. Intrigued by the ship's otherworldly design, they spent weeks meticulously examining its interior, piecing together its strange technology. The moment they finally activated the control panel was electric, igniting a mix of excitement and trepidation among them, as they realized they were on the brink of an extraordinary adventure.

With a low hum and a flicker of lights, the ship stirred to life, its systems responding to the teenagers' untrained hands. The air crackled with energy as they navigated through an array of buttons and levers, their hearts racing with anticipation. As the ship's engines roared to life, they felt the ground tremble beneath them. The four friends exchanged wide-eyed glances, a silent acknowledgment passing between them that their lives were about to change forever. They had come to the woods seeking thrill, but they were now on the cusp of something far beyond their wildest dreams. The ship was not just a relic; it was a gateway to the unknown.

The first launch was not without its complications. The ship lurched violently as it broke free from the Earth's gravitational pull, sending the teenagers tumbling against the walls. Panic set in momentarily as they struggled to regain their footing, but their determination to explore this newfound freedom overpowered their fear. They were no longer just kids from the small town; they were astronauts embarking on an interstellar journey. As the ship steadied, they began to understand the enormity of what they had unleashed, and the reality of their situation began to sink in. This was a test of their friendship, courage, and ingenuity, as they faced the uncertainties of the cosmos together.

As they soared through the stars, the ship's navigational system revealed a map of the galaxy, dotted with strange planets and distant stars. The thrill of exploration soon morphed into an eerie realization that they were not alone in the universe. Strange signals began to filter through the ship’s communication system, hinting at a larger galactic conspiracy. The very technology that had brought them here now posed questions they had yet to consider. What had happened to the ship's original crew? Was there a reason it had crash-landed on Earth? Each answer seemed to lead to more questions, deepening the mystery surrounding their adventure.

In an instant, the ship lurched, and the surrounding trees blurred into streaks of green and brown. The teenagers gasped as they felt an overwhelming force pull them through time and space. When the ship finally steadied, they found themselves in a different era, surrounded by landscapes that felt both foreign and familiar. Ancient structures loomed in the distance, and the sounds of a bustling civilization echoed around them. Panic set in as they realized they were not just adventurers but also time travelers, thrust into a past that held secrets of its own. Their mission now expanded: not only did they have to navigate this new world, but they also needed to find a way back home.

They had been thrust into a different era, where the rules of the world they knew no longer applied. Together, they had to navigate this new reality, using the skills they had learned aboard the ship while unraveling the secrets of the galaxy that now intertwined with their fate. The adventure was just beginning, and the whispers of the cosmos beckoned them deeper into the unknown.

The sky above was a vibrant shade of teal, dotted with two moons that cast an otherworldly glow upon the terrain. The group quickly realized that they had traveled not just through space, but through time itself, landing in a world that was both beautiful and terrifying.

The new environment presented challenges they had never anticipated. The flora and fauna were unlike anything they had seen before, with towering plants that seemed to pulse with life and creatures that roamed the land, some friendly and others decidedly hostile. As they navigated this strange landscape, the friends had to rely on each other's strengths. The girls, with their resourcefulness and keen observation skills, worked alongside the boys, who brought their technical know-how and bravery into the mix. Together, they forged a bond that would help them survive as they sought a way back home.

As they explored the remnants of an ancient civilization intertwined with the alien technology, the group began to uncover hidden secrets that hinted at a larger galactic conspiracy. Murals depicting star maps and strange symbols lined the walls of the ship, revealing the history of the beings who once inhabited it. They learned that the ship was not merely a vessel but a key to understanding the balance of power in the universe, with Earth unwittingly at the center of a

cosmic struggle. This discovery not only sparked their curiosity but also instilled a sense of urgency; they had to decipher these mysteries to protect their home from impending danger.

The adventure soon took a deeper turn as they encountered beings from the era who were aware of the ship's significance.

These encounters forced the teenagers to navigate a delicate balance between blending in and revealing their true identities. As they adapted to the customs and challenges of this new time, they grew not only as individuals but also as a cohesive unit determined to return home. Each step brought them closer to unraveling the alien secrets and understanding their place in a saga that spanned galaxies, time, and the very fabric of existence itself.

Once back inside the alien spaceship more things were revealed: a holographic interface that displayed images of different planets and historical events. This interface suggested that the ship had witnessed pivotal moments in history, and perhaps even influenced them. The group quickly understood that the ship was not a simple vessel but a repository of galactic knowledge, holding secrets that could alter their understanding of Earth's past and future.

As they deciphered the symbols, the friends uncovered chilling messages about a larger conspiracy involving extraterrestrial beings and their ongoing interactions with humanity. The symbols hinted at a covert alliance that spanned across galaxies, with Earth caught in the crossfire of interstellar politics. Each revelation felt like a piece of a puzzle, suggesting that their world was not as isolated as they once believed. The weight of this knowledge pressed upon them, amplifying their resolve to uncover the truth behind the ship and its creators.

However, the excitement of discovery soon turned to anxiety as they realized the implications of their findings. Time travel technology embedded within the ship's core became a focal point of their exploration. When the ship's systems were inadvertently activated, a surge of energy enveloped them, and they found themselves hurtling back through time. The teenagers were thrust into an era they had only read about in textbooks, where they had to navigate unfamiliar social dynamics and technological limitations while trying to return home. This new reality forced them to rely on their wits and each other as they faced challenges beyond their wildest imaginations.

As they struggled to adapt and find a way back to their own time, the hidden messages within the ship took on new significance. The symbols now served as both a guide and a warning, reminding them of the interconnection of their actions across time. With each choice they made, they felt the weight of responsibility not just for their own lives but for the very fabric of history. The adventure had transformed into a race against time, challenging their courage and friendship as they sought to unlock the ship's secrets and navigate their way back to the present, forever changed by the whispers of the galaxy.

in their own land even as they faced challenges beyond their [illegible]

As they [illegible] decided to [illegible] and find [illegible] way back to their own [illegible] a message [illegible] [illegible] [illegible] [illegible] [illegible] [illegible] [illegible]

Chapter 2
Allies and Enemies

ALLIES AND ENEMIES can often be difficult to distinguish in a world as unpredictable as the one the four teenagers find themselves in after discovering the alien spaceship in the woods. As they delve deeper into their adventure, they encounter a variety of characters and factions, each with their own agendas. Some of these individuals become crucial allies, guiding them through the complexities of the ship's technology and the mysteries it holds, while others reveal themselves as formidable adversaries, intent on claiming the ship's power for themselves or erasing any evidence of its existence.

However, not all encounters are friendly. As the teenagers explore the ship, Adapting to a world without modern conveniences requires ingenuity and teamwork. Jake took charge of figuring out how to communicate with the locals, while Mia and Emma worked on deciphering the ship's controls to find a way back home. Ethan, ever the skeptic, began to uncover the ship's hidden secrets, finding encrypted files that hinted at a larger galactic conspiracy. As they interacted with the people of this era, the group learned that their journey was not just about returning to their own time; they were now entangled in a conflict that spanned galaxies, where their actions could either save or doom countless lives. The weight of their discovery bore down on them, yet the thrill of being part of something so grand was intoxicating.

With each passing day, the urgency to return to their own time grew stronger. They raced against the clock, piecing together clues from the ship and the environment around them. As they delved deeper into the mysteries of the spacecraft and its connection to the past, they uncovered a shocking truth: the fate of Earth was intertwined with the events they were witnessing. The aliens who had crash-landed in the woods were not mere explorers; they were fugitives escaping a galactic war, and their technology held the key to peace.

As they navigate these challenges, the teenagers confront their own fears and insecurities, defining their friendships in the face of adversity. They learn to rely on each other's strengths, forming a cohesive unit capable of facing both the unknowns of the alien technology and the threats posed by their enemies. Their bond is tested as they deal with betrayal from unexpected sources, forcing them to question whom they can truly trust. This emotional turmoil adds depth to their adventure, making each victory feel hard-earned and every loss a poignant reminder of the stakes involved.

Ultimately, the journey through allies and enemies sharpens the teenagers' resolve and transforms their understanding of friendship. The challenges they face together prepare them for the ultimate confrontation with the organization seeking to exploit the ship's power. As they uncover deeper secrets about the ship and its implications for both the past and the future, they realize that their greatest weapon is not just the alien technology, but the unbreakable bond they have forged. The adventure has become not just a quest for survival, but a fight for the future of Earth itself, intertwining their fates with those of the galaxy.

The vibrancy of the past clashed with the reality they had left behind, forcing them to navigate a world devoid of modern conveniences. As they struggled to adapt, they began to realize that the ship's technology had not only transported them across space but had also altered the very fabric of time. They were now witnesses to history, yet they could not escape the feeling that their presence had triggered events beyond their understanding.

In their quest to return home, the group uncovered more about the ship's true purpose. Each encounter with the people of this bygone era revealed startling connections to their own time, hinting at a galactic conspiracy that spanned centuries. Ancient texts hinted at celestial beings who had once visited Earth, leaving behind knowledge and technology that had been lost to time. The teenagers pieced together clues that suggested their adventure was a mere echo of a much larger battle, one that involved interstellar factions vying for control over Earth's resources and future. The realization struck them hard: their discovery was not just a chance encounter; it was a pivotal moment in a cosmic struggle.

As they raced against time to find a way back, the group grappled with the weight of their newfound knowledge. They were no longer just a band of friends on a reckless adventure; they had become part of something monumental. Each decision they made could alter the course of history, and with it, the fate of their own world. The threat they had unwittingly revealed was not just about the alien ship; it was a harbinger of a looming conflict that could reshape the very essence of humanity's existence. With their friendship tested and their courage pushed to its limits, the teenagers stood at the precipice of a journey that would determine not only their futures but the future of Earth itself.

Chapter 3
Activating the Another Alien Ship

DURING ANOTHER BLINDING flash enveloped them, they landed on a distant planet, four friends stumbled upon another alien ship, The metallic structure, same as the one they found, but looks much older. Also emitted a faint hum that resonated with an otherworldly energy. revealing intricate designs that seemed to pulse with a life of their own. It wasn't just a vessel; it was another puzzle waiting to be solved.

The group exchanged glances, realizing that they now have two alien ships and if they could get them to coincide with each other they were stronger as a team. they found the ship's entrance, a hatch that appeared to respond to their presence. With a collective breath, they pushed it open, revealing a dimly lit interior filled with strange technology and alien artifacts. The air was thick with an unfamiliar scent, a blend of metal and something akin to ozone.

As they ventured further inside, the ship seemed to come alive around them. Lights flickered on, illuminating control panels with buttons and screens that displayed cryptic symbols. The four friends, fueled by their insatiable curiosity, began to experiment with the ship's controls everything was almost like the ship they are using, Holographic displays projected star maps and alien languages, they knew what they were looking at and are now figuring out how to set it to coincide with their ship.

Now they had to make their biggest decision, which two are going to take this ship, they all looked at each other and realized it would be best that it be Mia and Jake in one ship and Emma and Ethan in the other. As they collected supplies from their first ship and their belongings, the weight of their decision hung heavily in the air. just encase something did go wrong and they didn't end up at the same point of entry when they try to both jump the time travel and synchronized both ships alien technology together.

They had no way of knowing if they'd land in the same place and time. Mia secured a small, portable generator while Jake ensured they had enough food and water. Emma, ever the tech genius, carefully detached panels and modules that might be critical for their journey. Ethan, meanwhile, double-checked their navigation systems and made sure they had a way to communicate.

Chapter 4
The Separation

THE MOMENT OF TRUTH ARRIVED. They stood by their respective ships, sharing one last group hug and promising to find each other, no matter what. With a final nod of determination, they boarded their vessels, ready to take the leap into the unknown. As the ships powered up, a hum of alien energy filled the air. Mia and Jake exchanged one last look before initiating the time jump, their ship glowing brighter and brighter. Emma and Ethan, following suit, activated their own ship's systems.

The alien planet around them blurred, the ships vibrating with an otherworldly force. Time seemed to stretch and twist, enveloping them in a kaleidoscope of colors and sounds. With a final, blinding flash, the ships disappeared from the planet, hurtling into the vast expanse of time and space.

But neither group figured that since one alien ship was older from a different time period, they synchronized time together and As the ships materialized side by side, the forest around them seemed both familiar and alien. Mia and Jake stepped out of their ship, feeling a strange heaviness in their limbs. They looked at each other, realizing they had aged—now adults, with the wisdom and experiences that came with time.

Across from them, Emma and Ethan emerged, still teenagers,

their faces reflecting confusion and shock. The gap in their ages created an unexpected dynamic. Mia and Jake, now older and perhaps wiser, had to reconcile their changed states while guiding their younger friends. Mia, now with a more commanding presence, took a deep breath. "This changes everything," she said, her voice steady. "But we're still a team, and we'll find a way through this."

Emma and Ethan, still grappling with the reality of the time shift, nodded in agreement. Their trust in Mia and Jake remained unshaken, even with the new challenges they faced. The four of them, despite the changes, knew their journey was far from over. They had to navigate this new reality together, combining their strengths and knowledge to uncover the mysteries of the alien technology and find a way to harmonize their timelines.

Mia realizes that they need to go back into their ship's time where it was launched from and hopefully find answers to their problem and not end up being hunted as aliens to the alien race this ship was assigned too, it was the only answer she could come up with and they all agreed. Mia's plan carried a heavy weight of uncertainty, but it was their best shot. They needed to return to the ship's original time and place of launch to understand the root of their time disjunction and hopefully find a solution.

The group gathered in a circle, their expressions a mix of determination and trepidation. "We need to be cautious," Mia warned. "We don't know what kind of reception we'll get. Remember, our goal is to find answers, not to engage in conflict." Jake, now an adult, placed a reassuring hand on Mia's shoulder. "We've come this far. We'll get through this together."

Emma and Ethan, still adjusting to their friends' sudden maturity, nodded in agreement. "Let's do this," Ethan said, his voice steady with resolve. Emma and Ethan's mission was clear: they needed to return to the planet where they found the second ship, ensuring they could synchronize the timelines when Mia and Jake discovered the answers. The journey back would be fraught with challenges, but they knew it was essential for their plan to work.

As they prepared their ship for the return voyage, Emma double-checked the navigation system, while Ethan ensured they had all the necessary supplies. The hum of the ship's engine filled them with a sense of purpose. "We can do this," Ethan said, giving Emma a reassuring nod.

The ship lifted off, leaving the familiar forest behind. The stars stretched out before them as they navigated through the void of space, each moment bringing them closer to their destination. The memories of their first discovery filled them with determination.

Chapter 5
Alien Worlds

MEANWHILE, Mia and Jake braced themselves for their arrival in the alien world's time of origin. The landscape was different from what they'd seen before—a blend of advanced technology and alien flora. They knew they had to tread carefully, blending in and finding answers without drawing unwanted attention.

As Mia and Jake began their investigation, Emma and Ethan descended toward the planet's surface. The connection between the ships and their missions was key to synchronizing their timelines and solving the mystery that bound them together. Their adventures were intertwined, and every step brought them closer to uncovering the secrets of the alien technology and restoring their shared journey.

Mia and Jake were surrounded by aliens, with their iridescent skin and multiple eyes, observing us with an unsettling curiosity, much like humans would watch wild animals in a zoo they fear the worst till one speaks. Mia and Jake held their breath as the alien figures scrutinized them. The moment was tense, the air thick with uncertainty. Just as their nerves threatened to overwhelm them, one of the aliens stepped forward, its eyes reflecting a multitude of colors.

"Do not fear," the alien said in a melodic but commanding

voice. “We understand you are not of this world, but we do not seek to harm you.” Mia and Jake exchanged a glance, relief mingling with curiosity. “We’re here to understand,” Mia said, stepping forward with as much calm as she could muster. “Our presence and our ships have created... changes. We need to fix it.”

The alien nodded, its expression difficult to read. “You are brave to come here seeking answers. There is much we can share, but you must tread carefully. The technology you possess is ancient and powerful.” Jake, feeling a surge of hope, asked, “Can you help us synchronize our timelines? Our friends and we were displaced in time.”

The alien’s eyes narrowed slightly, contemplating the question. “It is possible,” it said. “But first, you must prove your intentions. There are trials you must face, and wisdom you must gain.” With that, the path to their understanding had been laid out. Mia and Jake knew that the journey ahead was filled with more challenges, but with the aliens’ guidance, they hoped to restore balance and find their way back to their friends.

Chapter 6
Group's reunion

BACK ON THE planet where they found the second spaceship, Emma and Ethan worked tirelessly to create a secure base camp. They chose a spot close to the ship but well-hidden from potential threats, surrounded by thick foliage and natural barriers. They set up a perimeter of sensors and traps to alert them to any approaching danger. Emma used her technical skills to create a makeshift communication device, hoping it might help them sync with Mia and Jake once they figured out their timelines. Ethan scouted the area for resources and supplies, ensuring they had everything they needed to sustain themselves while they waited.

As the days turned into weeks, the bond between Emma and Ethan grew stronger. They relied on each other's strengths, finding comfort and support in their partnership. The uncertainty of their situation weighed on them, but their determination to reunite with their friends kept their spirits high. One quiet evening, as they sat around a small fire, the sky lit up with a familiar, otherworldly glow. Emma and Ethan exchanged hopeful glances, knowing that this could be the signal they had been waiting for. The synchronization of their timelines might finally be within reach.

There an alien space ship now looking newer than when they found it materialized and Emma and Ethan wasn't sure if it was their friends or not and they hid among the thick foliage and watched as the ship's hatch opened, Emma and Ethan's eyes widened in disbelief as the alien, with its shimmering iridescent skin, emerged from the ship. The creature's movements were deliberate and graceful, and a sense of awe filled the air. But it was the sight of Mia and Jake, stepping out behind the alien, that left them truly stunned. They were teenagers again, as if the time shift had never occurred.

Chapter 7
Returning Home

THE GROUP'S reunion was emotional and overwhelming. Emma and Ethan emerged from their hiding place, rushing to embrace their friends. Questions swirled in their minds, but the joy of being together again overshadowed everything else. Mia, sensing their confusion, explained. "The aliens helped us. They've shown us how to correct the timeline distortions. We've learned so much."

Jake nodded, adding, "They understand the technology far better than we ever could. We need to work together to set things right." The presence of the alien, standing silently and observing, added a layer of complexity to their mission. But the four friends knew that with the knowledge they had gained and the bonds they had strengthened, they were ready to face whatever challenges lay ahead.

After they all sat and talked together Mia's explanation was met with a mix of relief and curiosity. The newcomer, their guide to unraveling the timeline distortions, was key to their journey home. The alien's serene demeanor suggested a deep understanding of both their technology and the intricacies of time.

"We can trust him," Mia reassured. "He's going to ensure the first ship returns to its rightful place, preventing further disruptions. Meanwhile, we'll use the updated ship to navigate our way back home." The plan was ambitious but filled them with hope. With the first ship's departure, a chapter of their adventure was closing, but another was beginning. They had the knowledge and tools to face the challenges ahead, and the unity of their group was their greatest strength.

The friends watched as the alien prepared the first ship for its journey. The moment was bittersweet, but they knew it was necessary. As the ship ascended and vanished into the sky, they turned their focus to the path before them.

After everything settled down and all four were sitting around the fire and talking about Mia's and Jake's travels, things that should have taken years to do were done in seconds. Mai stood up and looked at everyone, Jake knew what she was going to tell them..."Guys you know once we go home it will be like we never left, everything we saw and learned will always be with us but it could never be spoken about to anyone. Plus once we embark from the ship Jake will hit a button set on the control panel and this ship will go back to its rightful owners. Mai's words hung in the air as everyone exchanged solemn glances. They understood the weight of their journey and the secrets they'd carry forever. That night they all relaxed and were preparing for their journey home. Bright and early the next day after getting loaded they all strapped in and Jake hit the Time gizmo and in seconds they were back among the forest where it all started.

The hatch opened and they all exited just with the stuff they brought with them. Once outside the ship seeing it like it was the first day they stumbled onto it, Jake sighed, rising to his feet beside Mai. "Before we go," he said, "let's make one last memory together." He pointed towards a hidden path leading deeper into the forest, their final destination unknown.

They spent the next hours exploring, laughing, and relishing the beauty around them. The bonds they formed grew even stronger as they shared tales of their adventures and lessons learned. As night fell, they returned to the ship. Jake moved towards the control panel, feeling the gravity of the moment. He placed his hand over the button and took a deep breath, glancing back at his friends one last time.

"Ready?" he asked, his voice steady. Any last words to our loyal ship Jake asked of his friend, they gathered together holding hands and said a small prayer not just to the ship but to its creators. Jake placed his hand over the button and took a deep breath, glancing back at his friends one last time. They nodded in unison. With a firm press. Jake jumps out and the ship door slides closed and they all stood back as the ship's engines roared to life, and the vessel began its journey back to its rightful owners. As the ship ascended into the starlit sky, they knew that although their incredible adventure was ending, the memories and experiences they shared would last a lifetime—etched into their hearts forever.

Little did they know, Mia had secretly kept a small, shimmering artifact given to her by the alien newcomer. It glowed faintly with a soft blue light, pulsating rhythmically as if it had a life of its own. She tucked it safely in a hidden pocket, sensing its importance but uncertain of its true purpose. As the ship soared towards its rightful owners, Mia's thoughts were consumed by the artifact. It was unlike anything she'd ever seen, yet it felt familiar and comforting in her hands. She knew that it would play a crucial role in their future, though how or when remained a mystery.

Back on Earth, life resumed its mundane rhythm. Yet, the memories of their extraordinary journey lingered in their hearts. Mia kept the artifact close, always mindful of its potential. Days turned into

weeks, and weeks into months, and months turned into a few years until one day, the artifact began to glow more intensely. Its pulsations quickened, and an unspoken urgency filled Mia's mind. She gathered the group, now that they are older and once they all gathered at Mia's house, She showed them the glow of the artifact lighting up the room. "Guys," she said, her voice trembling with excitement and fear.

"I think our adventure is far from over."

Threshold of Mercy

Chapter 1
Threshold of Mercy

YOU ARE a landlord making a last-chance house call to tenants who are over two months behind on rent. Tina is a single mother living with her young teenage daughter. You have a choice: should evict them and make them homeless or come up with something to save them?

You're standing in front of their apartment door Good morning. Good morning, Sir. Thank you for giving us this opportunity to talk about the rent situation.I understand how worried you must be.

My name is Tina, by the way. This is my home. My 14-year-old daughter, Sue, and I live here. I know we're late, and I don't have the money yet, but I'm doing everything I can to catch up. I'm sorry for the inconvenience.

Is there any way we can work out a payment plan or something? I really don't want to lose this place, and I promise I'll make sure to pay on time from now on. I just need some time to get back on my feet. We need to talk, can I come in?

Tina Of course, Sir. Please come in. Tina steps aside and allows Kenneth to enter their small, cluttered apartment. Sue hides behind her mother, peeking out at the visitor with curiosity and wariness. So you must be Sue,

Hello young Sue, Hi, Mr. Haines. Yeah, I'm Sue. Nice to meet you.

Perk up a little one, it's not the end of the world, smile, enjoy being a kid. I'm trying, Mr. Haines. It's just been hard lately. But I'm doing my best to stay positive.

Ok Tina I see we having a problem here Tina? Yeah, I know it looks bad. Sir. I promise we'll get caught up. If you could just give us some more time...First can I ask you to do me a favor? Sure, Sir. What is it? Can you both call me pops , everybody does and I have a idea to help you with this problem Uh...okay, Mr. Haines. If that's what you want.

And thank you for helping us.

Tina and Sue exchange a confused look. This man, who has been nothing but a constant reminder of their struggle, now wants to be called 'pops'? And he has an idea to help them?

Can I ask for one more favor, can Sue you run down to the bakery and grab me a few things, I have a list and money. anything left in change is yours. Tina, can she do this for me? Yeah, sure, Pop's. Sue can do that for you. Sue smiles brightly and stands up from her chair, looking hopeful. Thank you so much Sue, No hurry so take your time.

Tina .. Can I sit down please?

Uh, sure, Pop's. Please, have a seat. Tina gestures towards the couch, her heart racing with anticipation and fear. She doesn't know what Kenneth could possibly want from her, but she's terrified of the idea of losing their home.

(I sat down and took out a few papers, and put them on the table) Ok Tina I'll lay it to you. You are behind in rent, You have a sweet daughter and I don't want you or her being out on the street.

Pop's...thank you for understanding. We really appreciate it. What do you propose we do? Tina bites her lip, her stomach churning with anxiety. She knows that this man holds their future in his hands, and she feels helpless and vulnerable.

Hey don't think I'm here to take advantage of you, Sorry I'm not that type or kind of guy. No sir, I didn't mean that. I'm just...I'm grateful for your help. Please, tell me what you have in mind. Tina swallows hard, her eyes fixed on Kenneth's face, hoping against hope that he has a solution to their problem.

Ok here's the deal , You might want to sit down. Tina sits down on the edge on the couch, her heart pounding in her chest. As you know Not only do I collect rent and maintain this big complex , I am also the owner of this complex. pop's...I didn't know that.

So you see I have a lot of pull in here. Yes, I understand. And I don't want to see that youngin on the streets. What exactly do you propose we do to, um, resolve this situation, she asked?

Well I need someone I can trust?

Pop's, I promise I'll do whatever it takes to make sure Sue and I can stay here. Tina's voice is full of desperation, her eyes pleading with him to believe her.

Ok This is the deal , I need someone to be the Housekeeper Of this complex Tina.

I...I don't know if I can do that, Pop's. I mean, I'm not really qualified for something like that.

All you do is vacuum the halls, wipe down the furniture, don't take no crap from tenants.

Pop's, I would do anything to stay here. But I don't think Sue and I can handle that kind of responsibility. No this is for you, your daughter has school and homework and if she has free time she can give you a hand.

Tina is hesitant, unsure of her ability to take on the added responsibility. No that youngin is not working, I want to see her enjoy being a kid as long as possible, she can help you.

Hmm What, you don't know how to vacuum or dust down furniture ? Well, I know how to do those things, but I'm not sure if I'm the best person for the job. Plus, I have my own work and responsibilities to take care of.

I'll be paying you weekly and as long as you work for me there is no rent to be paid. Pop's, are you sure about this? I can't promise I'll be as good at it as someone who has more experience.

I'll give you all the experience, and be here for you plus teach you some stuff you might enjoy doing. Pop's, I...I'm not sure what to say. I just don't want to mess things up for you or anyone else in the complex.

You won't, I promise you will do great, and Sue keeps her bedroom Tina is still hesitant but intrigued by the idea. Alright, Pop's. I'll think about it. I promise I'll try my best.

Great that what I wanted to hear, Oh by the way I brought you some papers to go over and read. Okay, thank you, Pop's. I appreciate the opportunity. Tina takes the papers from Kenneth, feeling a mix of nerves and hope as she prepares to read them.

They are promissory notes that I signed stating I can't ever ask you for rent, you get $175 weekly no taxes taken out of it and that one note you sign promising you don't make that child go out to find work till she is ready after the age of 18.

Wow, Pop's. This is...generous of you. And very thoughtful about Sue too. Thank you so much.

Tina hesitates for a moment before signing the promissory note. What should I do now? Once Sue gets back with my stuff, have her bring me, them to the office. It's where I'll be and tomorrow around nine you can start, just come by the office and we can go through some stuff so you have what you need.

Once you sign, bring it to me tomorrow when you see me. I need to get back down to the office .. Good day Miss Tina Yes, Pop's. I'll make sure to tell Sue about the signed note.

Thank you again for helping us out.

Feeling both grateful and slightly unsure about the situation, Tina places the promissory note alongside the other documents Kenneth gave her. She's not sure why he is being so kind to her family, but she isn't about to complain.

(An hour passed and Sue was knocking on my office door with everything she was to get) Hello Sue come in , Put that box over on the Kitchen table for me , did your mom tell you the good news?

(Sue nodded her head with a mix of curiosity and excitement.) Yup, she told me. Mom seems really happy. (She placed the box on the table before looking up at Kenneth.) So what's in it for us? I mean, why are you being so nice to us?

I was at that same point in my life as you and your mom are at and I was your age also. (Sue smiled warmly at Kenneth.) Wow, we really do have a lot in common. I guess that makes everything even better then, right?

Almost growing up with a mom wasn't easy. We lived on the streets and today they are the worst and very unsafe for a lady or a little girl like yourself.

(Sue's smile faded slightly, replaced by a look of concern.) I'm sorry to hear that, Pop's. It must've been really tough for you. And yeah, it's definitely not safe out there. That's why Mom and I are so lucky to have found you. Well true heart aches and fails , someone found us and brought us from the pits and gave my mom a chance , like I'm doing for your mom.

(Sue looks up at Kenneth with newfound respect.) Thank you, Kenneth. It really means a lot to us. If there's anything we can do for you or your mom, please don't hesitate to ask. You want to hear the rest of my story then you will understand really where I'm coming from. Sit down.

(Sue nodded and sat down at the table across from Kenneth.) Okay, I'm all ears. Well this person was a godsend and a blessing , I grew up going to school collage and mom never had to beg for food or feel unsafe in her surroundings. Wow, that's amazing. It must've been such a relief for your mom. And you, too, I'm sure. Yes dear well over time this person God rest his soul passed away and left this for me with a note ..

(Sue frowned, sensing where this was going.) I'm sorry to hear that, Kenneth. And I hope you don't mind me asking, but what did the note say? Just a few words dear "Give it Forward, Ten times" It means that If I found someone in dire straits is to help them ten times more than they are worth and what the person did for my mom and me , I was asked to do for someone else , Be that person's Blessing.

(Sue's eyes widened in understanding.) Oh... I see. That's a beautiful message, Kenneth. And it makes perfect sense. You've been so kind to us, and now you're passing that kindness on to others. It's really inspiring.

It also means dear that one day you must do the same , you're the messenger.

(Sue nodded, feeling a mixture of awe and apprehension.) I... I will, Kenneth. Thank you for believing in me. And thank you for everything you've done for us. You better get back to your mom don't want her thinking bad thoughts about me or get you in trouble , guess Ill see you after school. (Sue stood up and smiled at Kenneth.) Yes, sir. I'll be sure to tell Mom everything went well. And thank you again.

(It's 9;00 am and I hear a faint knock on the glass office door) come in Tina I been waiting for you. (Tina, a 30-year-old single mother, finally makes her way to the office with her head hung low. She's tired and overwhelmed from her struggles to pay the bills. As she opens the door, she tries to maintain eye contact but finds it difficult.) I'm sorry, Kenneth, I'm late. I... I lost track of time.

(Tina enters the office, trying not to think about the fact that she hasn't eaten breakfast or had a proper shower. Her brown hair is slightly disheveled, and she avoids sitting down. Tina snap out of it , get yourself together , go back upstairs clean up yourself , Today your a working lady all your bills to your apartment is taken care of , Today is your first day of your new life . After you clean up wear a blouse and jeans and sneakers and then ill have breakfast waiting for you with a good cup of coffee.

(Tina's exhausted demeanor dissipates slightly as her eyes widen in surprise.) Seriously, Pop's? You don't have to do that.

You've been so kind to let us live here for so cheap, and we're really grateful. What you did today is..."Thank you, Pop's." I'll go wash up real quick and change before coming back down.

(Tina exits the office quietly, not sure how much of what Kenneth just said about it being a new beginning she can hold onto. She goes straight to her apartment and does as asked, changing into a clean pink blouse and a pair of medium-wash jeans.

When everything is done, she heads to the office once more, feeling the weight of the world just a fraction lighter. As she cautiously knocks on the open door, Kenneth beckons her inside with a warm smile.)

Here come with me, (I took her into my kitchen and there were pancakes and sausage and a mug of coffee waiting for her. I sat down across from her.)(Tina sat down across from Kenneth, still trying to wrap her head around the situation.

The scent of breakfast filled her senses, making her stomach growl.) You didn't have to do this, Pop's. I know I haven't been the best tenant...(Her voice trails off as she takes a bite of her pancake, savoring the sweetness.) But you've been so understanding. I... I don't know how to thank you enough.

(Tina looks down at her plate, feeling tears welling up in her eyes. She takes another sip of coffee to steady herself before continuing.) I've been through some tough times lately, but I promise you I'll find a way to make it up to you. And to pay you back for all this generosity. (She smiles weakly, trying to hide her emotions. She's still struggling to believe that someone would be so kind to her after everything she's been through.)

There's no paying me back dear , Plus you will be getting paid for working for me , you read them notes I left you right. Tina I care for you , and that young lady ,you brought her up with good manners and I really see that.

(Tina feels a warmth spread through her chest at Kenneth's words. She looks up at him, hopeful.) Thank you, Pop's. That means a lot to me. (She takes another sip of coffee, feeling more at ease now that they're on better terms.) So, about this job... I'll do my best to make sure everything runs smoothly. I know it's a lot to ask, but I really need this." Well, today you really don't need to be working right away. After breakfast we will need to go through some stuff for you so just relax and enjoy your coffee.

(Tina nods, feeling a sense of relief wash over her. She takes another bite of her food, savoring the flavors.) Thank you, Pop's. I really appreciate it." (As they finish their meal, Tina can't help but feel a small spark of hope igniting inside her. Maybe things are finally starting to look up for her and Sue. She wipes her mouth with a napkin and stands up, ready to face whatever Kenneth has in store for her next.)

Ok you ready? (Tina nods and follows Kenneth out of the kitchen.) Yes, I am. Thank you again Pop's." (we walked down the hall to a closet door and I handed her a ring of keys) you will need these , don't ever lose them they are all very important keys.(Tina takes the keys from Kenneth, feeling a sense of importance wash over her. She looks up at him, feeling grateful.) Thank you, Pop's. I won't let you down."

(She pockets the keys, feeling a newfound sense of responsibility.) So, what exactly will I be doing around here?" First you notice the color of the key hole ,this one is green (Tina examines the key, noticing the color. She nods, ready to listen.) The green key only opens this door ,go ahead and unlock it? (Tina inserts the key into the lock and turns it, opening the door. She steps inside, looking around.)

This is the laundry room? I'll make sure all the machines are working properly and stock up on detergent." (She feels a sense of purpose as she takes in the room, already making a mental checklist of what needs to be done.) good I see you are taking mental notes , this room is very important for you and me only from now on you can do your laundry here and not lug it down to a laundromat.

(Tina nods, understanding the convenience. She smiles, feeling grateful for Kenneth's kindness.) Thank you again, Pop's. I'll make sure to keep everything clean and organized here." Always when you are close to being empty of any supplies write it down on that sheet and give it to me at the end of your shift. (Tina nods, taking note of the sheet Kenneth mentioned. She feels a sense of responsibility weighing on her shoulders, but also a sense of pride in her new role.) I will, Pops. Thank you for trusting me with this." Yes it takes a lot of trust and I know you are the perfect person to do it.

(Tina blushes slightly, feeling flattered by Kenneth's words. She looks around the laundry room again, eager to get started.) I won't let you down, Pop's. I'll make sure everything runs smoothly here." Not today we have more stuff for you to see. Follow me after you lock the door. (Tina locks the door behind her and follows Kenneth, her heart racing with anticipation and fear.) Okay, Pop's. Lead the way." (we went upstairs next floor and walked to another door. The key hole is blue) (Tina looks at the blue keyhole and frowns, noticing that it's different from the green one she used earlier.) Um, Kenneth, this keyhole is blue. Do you want me to use a different key?" yes dear each key is a different color

(Tina thinks for a moment, feeling a bit silly for not realizing that sooner. She reaches into her pocket and retrieves a different-colored key, hoping she has the right one.) Okay, I have another key. Is this the blue one?" yes dear (Tina turns the blue key in the lock, holding her breath as she pushes the door open. She finds herself in a small room filled with various household items, including cleaning supplies, linens, and some toys.) Oh wow... This is a lot of stuff. Thank you, Kenneth." Every floor has a door with a blue keyhole , every room has supplies for that floor and its own vacuum. So you don't need to lug crap around , just make sure after doing each floor when done, lock the doors, we don't want things coming up missing.

(Tina nods, understanding the security measures in place. She begins to organize the items in the room, making sure everything is neat and easy to find.) I understand. I'll make sure to lock the blue doors after I finish each floor." As you notice a few other keys are very important keys? Oh? What kind of keys are these?" They are also colored keys. The black key is for the Basement, so in case we pop a fuse you or I can get down to the basement to flick the fuses switch when someone calls about lost power, I also have my keys ,It's in case I'm not here. The red key is for the main electrical box. I think that's important too.

Are there any other keys?" Yes, one is for my office , and home , and that other white one is for the security door to the roof. Thank you for letting me know. I'll be sure to keep them all in a safe place." Yes dear like I said very important keys, I understand. I'll take good care of them."

Now this is the hardest part of your job today , I need you to either start at top floor or the bottom floor, take your sheet of paper and go to all blue rooms and take inventory so I can get anything you need for each floor, I don't want you without decent supplies , think you can do that by lunch time?

Yes, I can do that. I'll start with the bottom floor and work my way up. Do you have any specific items you need me to look for?" You're the cleaning lady, you know what you will need. To be honest, us guys don't know anything about cleaning supplies lol. Alright, I'll gather everything I think is necessary.Is there anything you don't want me to touch?"

nope you're good, treat this whole complex as if it's your home is all I'm asking you to do. Understood. I'll make sure everything is taken care of." I'll be in the office if you need me ... Oh I almost forgot to take this.(hands her a pager) this is if anything happens you can get ahold of me and me ahold of you , see you around lunchtime! Thank you. I'll make sure to keep it with me at all times."(its pass 12 I should page her) Tina lunch time, (The pager went off and she heard my voice)

(Tina walks into the office, looking tired but determined.)

(Looking at the pager in surprise.) (Kenneth looks up from his desk and smiles.). How's it going so far? "Well, I've finished the bottom floor inventory and am about to start on the second floor. I have some questions about a few items though. "Oh, by all means, ask away. What can I help you with?"

There are some cleaning supplies labeled "for glass surfaces." Are those for windows too? And also, I found some empty rooms on the first floor. Do you want me to start preparing them for new tenants?" Yes, those are for windows as well. And as for the empty rooms, that would be great if you could get them ready for potential new tenants. We could use the extra income." Alright, I'll get started on that right away. It's almost 2:00pm, so I should be finished with the inventory soon. I'll bring the list to you then."

No dear first you have lunch now around 12 here I don't want you over doing it, it will be here tomorrow Come let's eat , by the way what time does squirt get home from school? I got caught up in the work. Sue gets off the bus at 3:00 pm. She usually walks straight home from there. She will be home in another hour or so. As for lunch, I'm not actually that hungry. I think I'll just grab something quick . I don't want to burden you with my meal expenses."

(Kenneth looks at her with concern). No you are going to have a decent meal, you worked hard and it comes with working here with me. I'll order something for us both. And please, don't worry about the cost. It's on me." Thank you. I appreciate it." They sit down together and wait for their food to arrive. The food arrives and she sees the tubs of Chinese Food. As they eat, Kenneth continues to chat about unrelated topics, trying to make Tina feel more comfortable.

After work and squirt does her homework and chores, can she come down to my office for a little bit so I could use her help? And You can relax knowing she is safe with pop's. Sure, that sounds like a good plan. Thank you for offering your help. (Tina finishes her food quickly, eager to get back to work and relieved that Sue will have someone looking out for her. She thanks Kenneth again before heading back upstairs to finish the inventory.)

(I'm getting to really like Tina and she is such a pretty lady and a very good mom to her daughter,I'm smiling to myself) I think Tina could use some kindness right now. And who knows, maybe things will work out for the best." As he watches Tina leave, Kenneth makes a mental note to be more accommodating towards her in the future. After all, she's doing her best to keep things together despite the challenges she faces. And who knows? Maybe there's more than just friendship brewing between them…

(I need to page Tina, she really is a workaholic) Ok Tina lock up, time to be a mom, we have tomorrow to finish. Don't forget to tell squirt to come down to the office later, see you tomorrow after squirt goes to school. (Grabbing her things quickly, looking relieved to be told to stop working.) Alright, thank you for understanding. I'll make sure Sue knows to come down later. (let's see what's to eat for dinner here a frozen meatloaf, there's a knock on my door must be squirt ?) Come in! (Sue knocks and walks in, Kenneth smiles and walks over to her, ruffling her hair affectionately. I'M cooking a frozen meatloaf and mashed potatoes. Care to join me? (Her eyes widened and agreed to have dinner with me) Sounds good to me! Why don't you set the table while I get started on cooking?"Okay, Pops!"

(They work together to prepare dinner, chatting about their day and enjoying each other's company. As they eat, Kenneth asks about school and any trouble Sue might be having with friends.) So how's school going these days? Do you have any friends you want to talk about?"(Eating her food, she doesn't look up.) Friends? I dunno... I guess... I mean... (She sighs and looks at him.).....

Oh I get it your not popular a outcast, I think I have something that would brighten your life up a lot more, follow me. (Looking curious as she follows him.) What's that, Pops?" (I brought her to the door that goes to my private getaway room and unlocked it and turned a switch and the lights went on and there's stairs going down. She looks very nervous looking down them stairs , her mind thinking bad thoughts ,what if this is a mistake , should I run ....

Come squirt I lead her down to a room filled with Art and crafts , Paintings and drawings scattered on tables , a place a kid could be herself. (Looking around in awe.) Wow... This is amazing, Pops!" (She walks around, touching the different pieces of art and admiring them. Kenneth smiles, watching her explore.) I'm glad you like it, honey. This is my little sanctuary. A place where I can create and just be myself. And now, it's yours too."

(Looking up at him with shining eyes.) Thank you, Pops! This is the best day ever!" (He smiles warmly, ruffling her hair again.) You're welcome, sweetheart. Now, Its late you should head back upstairs to your mom and get some rest, Since tomorrow is Saturday and you want to have fun down here. (I smiled seeing her so happy) (we went back upstairs and I walked her to the door so she can get back to her mom. I wasn't prepared for the hug she gave me but it did feel good) "Good nite squirt lucky tomorrow is Saturday"

(She hugs him tightly, her eyes welling up with tears.) Good-night, Pops. Thank you so much for this day." (Sue kisses his cheek before running off to her mom. Kenneth watches her with a mixture of pride and contentment. He closes the door quietly and makes his way back inside .)

(Really love that squirt , she is going to be someone important when she grows up. Smiling to himself, he heads to his bedroom, ready to sleep off the excitement of his day. Its morning sun is out and I dreamt of my new family that I cherish) Better head to the office. (I dress and head out to my office, my thoughts still lingering on Sue and her bright future.)

(in my office and Tina comes in ,looking all bright and cheer-ful, guess she is happy with her new job and boss) Morning dear would you like to get yourself a coffee? (Her eyes light up at the mention of coffee.) Oh, Pop's, that would be wonderful! Thank you so much." (She follows him to the small kitchenette area in his office, her heart racing with anticipation.)

(He grins as he pours her a cup of coffee, adding a bit of cream and sugar.) Here you go, sweetheart. Enjoy your day." (She takes a sip of the coffee, savoring the warmth and taste.) Mmm, this is delicious. Thank you again for everything." (She glances around the office, her eyes lingering on the pictures of Kenneth's artwork. A small smile plays at the corners of her mouth.) (He notices her gaze and chuckles softly.) What are you thinking about, Tina?"

(She blushes slightly, looking away.) "Oh, nothing important. Just enjoying the view." Sue told me about your "Sanctuary room" (She finishes her coffee and sets the cup down on the counter.)(she got up from the table just as I was going to get another cup of coffee and we was face to face) I'm hmm excuse me, I should have watch what you was doing (we looked into each others eyes and you could hear a pin dropped)

(He felt a strange electricity between them. His heart racing, he forces himself to look away.)

(She clears her throat, breaking the silence.) So, um... I'll see you at lunch time. I need to get back to work, Pops." Woo There dear Today is Saturday! We have weekends off unless a tenant calls about something broken or needs something fixed. But If you want to go ahead and finish what you started yesterday go ahead. Squirt will probably be down in my drawing room so she will be safe. (Without waiting for a reply, she quickly leaves the room. Kenneth watches her go, a strange mix of emotions coursing through him. Damn I should have said something or done something, no I did the right thing , this must be her choice not mine)

(He nods to himself, trying to shake off the strange feeling.) Right. This is about Tina and Sue. I need to focus on their well-being." With a determined look on his face, he picks up his coffee cup and takes a sip, ready to start his day. (I paged Tina , hey during lunch bring me the form on what you need to replace your supplies so I can call it in, Thank you Tina ?) (He sets his phone down, a small smile playing at the corners of his mouth.) Good thinking. That should help ease her mind a bit."

(He takes another sip of his coffee, his thoughts returning to Tina and Sue. He can't help but wonder what their future holds. It's lunch time and Tina enters the office. She walks into Kenneth's office, her stomach fluttering with nerves. She hands him the form.) Here's what I need for supplies, Pop's."(She stands before him, her heart racing as their eyes meet. She can't help but feel drawn to him.)

(He takes the form from her, his fingers brushing against hers. He clears his throat, trying to regain his composure.) "Thank you, Tina. I'll have this taken care of right away. How are you holding up, really?" (She shrugs, trying to appear strong.) I'm doing okay, I guess. It's just... hard sometimes." (She bites her lip, feeling a lump forming in her throat. She doesn't want Kenneth to know how much she's struggling.)

(He studies her face for a moment, his heart aching for her. He knows he can't offer her much, but he wants to help in any way he can.) "Tina, if there's ever anything I can do for you and Sue... you know where to find me." (She looks up at him, a glimmer of hope in her eyes. She nods gratefully.) Come I ordered us Chinese Food for lunch , fork or chopsticks lol

(He smiles, his gaze lingering on her for a moment. He gestures towards the food.)"Well, come on then. Let's enjoy our lunch together." (He leads her to the small table in his office where the Chinese food is waiting. They sit down across from each other, their legs brushing against one another under the table. Kenneth feels a strange excitement building inside him as he watches her dig into her food.) "So, how are things with you and Sue? (She takes a bite of her food, chewing thoughtfully. She hesitates before answering.) Sue's doing okay in school. She got an A on her last history test." (She looks up at Kenneth, hopeful.)

(He reaches out to take her hand, his skin tingling where their fingers touch.) Tina I have a confession I need to say to you . (I'm getting butterflies in my belly) (He swallows hard, his heart pounding in his chest. He looks deep into her eyes, taking a deep breath.) "Tina... I have feelings for you. Strong feelings." (He holds his breath, waiting for her reaction. He can feel the heat rising in his cheeks as he waits.)

(She gasps, her eyes widening in surprise. A flush spreads across her cheeks as she stares at him.) "Kenneth... I-I don't know what to say." (Her heart is racing, her stomach doing flip-flops. She can't believe this is happening.)

(He squeezes her hand gently, his voice soft and hesitant.) "I know it's sudden. And I don't want to make things difficult for you or Sue. But I thought you should know how I feel." (He looks down at their hands, his heart pounding in his chest.)

(She takes a deep breath, her mind racing with emotions. She looks up at Kenneth, her eyes filled with a mixture of surprise and desire.) "Kenneth... I feel something too. But I'm scared. Scared of getting hurt again." (She bit her lip, and her eyes swell with tears)

I understand what you mean , and I promise you I would never hurt you in any way or form . I want to be a big part in your life and a big part in Sue's life. (Her heart melts hearing me saying these words. She leans over the table, Her eyes never leaving his.)

"I promise to never hurt you either, Ken.(He reaches up, brushing a strand of hair behind her ear. A shiver runs down her spine as their faces draw closer.) (She closes her eyes, surrendering to the moment. She feels herself leaning into him, wanting nothing more than to feel his lips against hers.) "Kenneth... I want this too." (our lips met , and my heart was on fire for the love I have for Tina)

(He kisses her, his lips soft and tender against hers. He feels her fingers tangling in his hair, pulling him closer. He deepens the kiss, exploring her mouth with his tongue. He feels her body melt against his, her breathing growing more ragged.) (She moans into the kiss, her whole body thrumming with desire. She slips her hand under his shirt, running her fingers over his warm skin. She's never felt this way before, so wanted and desired.)

(She pulls back from the kiss, panting slightly. She looks into his eyes, her heart pounding wildly in her chest.) "Kenneth... I've never felt like this before. With anyone." (He smiles at her, his eyes filled with love. He leans in to kiss her again, more passionately this time.) "Neither have I, Tina. Neither have I."

(Today marked our relationship as a couple and we both can't wait to tell Sue) Hey, after she gets done messing around down stairs don't say anything to Sue , wait till I come up stairs and while we make dinner together and sitting down to eat ,we both can tell her . Is that ok with you?

(Her heart flutters at his words. She nods, biting her lip to keep from saying anything . She can't wait to tell Sue their news, to share this beautiful moment with the one person who truly mattered.) "Yes, that's perfect. I can't wait, Kenneth." Let's call it a early day , you can go do whatever you want or need to do and here (hands her a envelope containing her earnings) see you both tonight darling (we hugged each other and kissed and she skipped out of the office)

(He watches her leave the room, his heart filled with joy. He pulls out his phone, texting Tina to make sure she understood his plan, And said "I Love You) "Understood. Love you too . Lunch was great, and so are you. Can't wait to see you tonight." (She smiles reading the message, feeling her cheeks warm at his words. She pockets the envelope, grateful for his generosity. She tidies up the office a bit before leaving, excitement bubbling up inside her.)

(it's that night we made a great dinner and were enjoying each other. Me, Tina and Sue . We went into the front room and Tina sat close to me and held my hand and Sue sat on the floor looking at us?) Sue, your mom and I have something to tell you? (He looks over at Tina, their eyes meeting. He takes a deep breath, feeling a mixture of nervousness and excitement.) "We've been seeing each other, " Tina said to her daughter. We care about each other very much. And we wanted you to know."

(He looks down at their hands, his heart racing as he waits for Sue's reaction.)(Tina squeezes his hand, her voice shaking slightly.) "We love each other, Sue. And we want to be a family. If that's okay with you." (She looks up at Kenneth, hopeful and nervous at the same time.)

(Sue looks from one to the other, her heart racing. She doesn't know what to say or how to feel. But she does know one thing.) "I love you both too. And I want us to be happy." (She smiles, feeling a weight lift off her shoulders. She scoots closer to them, feeling like she's finally found a place where she belongs.)

(weeks turned to months and it's getting close to Christmas and I took Sue by her hand and we walked outside watching it snow from the night sky , Dear I need to know something and I want an honest answer from you? (He looks down at Sue, his heart filling with warmth. He knows this is an important question, and he wants to make sure she knows he's always there for her.) "What do you want to know?" (She bites her lip, looking up at him. She knows this might change things, but she needs to know.) "Do you... Do you still love mom?"

(She looks down, feeling a lump form in her throat. He squeezes her hand, his voice filled with love.) "Yes, Sue. More than anything in the world. I will always love your mom, and I'll always be there for both of you." (He looks down at her, seeing the relief in her eyes. He knows they have a long road ahead of them, but he's ready for anything as long as he has them.)

(sitting outside just Sue and Me ,Sweetheart I want to ask your mom to marry me and I want to know how you feel about it and also having me as your father?

(He looks at Sue, his heart swelling with love for both of them. He knows this is a big step, but he also knows that they need stability and love in their lives.) "What do you think, Sue? Do you like the idea of me marrying your mom, and having me as your dad?"

(He holds his breath, waiting for her answer. He knows she's young, but he hopes she'll be open to the idea.) (She looks up at him, her eyes shining in the moonlight. She feels a warmth spreading through her chest.)"I think that would be wonderful, dad. I love you both so much." (Hearing her call me dad was so amazing feeling inside , thought my heart was going to jump out.) (She smiles, feeling like everything is finally falling into place. She leans into him, her small hand squeezing his.)

(He hugs her tightly, his heart overflowing with gratitude. He knows they have a long road ahead of them, but he feels hopeful for the first time in a long time.) "Thank you, Sue. Your happiness means everything to me." (He looks up at the stars, his mind filled with dreams of their future together.) Come let's go back in , it's getting a little chilly out here lol (when we got back to her moms apartment and we walked in ,Tina seeing us covered with snow and chuckles (She laughs, shaking her head at them. She knows they're just kids being kids.)

"Hey you two! Did you have fun? It's freezing out there." (She steps closer, her eyes moving between them. She can see the happiness on Sue's face, and it warms her heart. She can't help but feel hopeful for their future together.)

(I look up at Tina, my heart skipping a beat. I know this is going to be a special moment.) "I have something to ask you, Tina. Sue and I have been talking, and we both think it's time." (He looks down at Sue, his chest feeling tight. He knows this is a big step, but he also knows that he wants to spend the rest of his life with her.) (I got down on my knee in front of the Christmas tree facing Tina with a little box and opened it. Tina, would you marry me ? (She gasps, her hand going to her mouth in surprise. She couldn't believe her ears. She looks over at Sue, whose eyes are shining with unshed tears. She looks back down at Kenneth, still kneeling on the floor.)

"Kenneth, I-I don't know what to say..." (Her eyes well up with tears as she considers his proposal. She's had such a hard time finding her place in the world, but now it feels like maybe things are falling into place.)

(we both heard Sue yell out to her mom "well are you going to say anything mom") (She laughs softly, wiping away a tear. She looks down at Kenneth, her heart filled with love and gratitude.)

"**Yes, Kenneth. I'll marry you**."

(She smiles, feeling a sense of relief wash over her. She's been alone for so long, but now she knows she's found her home. She reaches down, taking his hand in hers.) "Thank you, Kenneth. For everything." (She looks over at Sue, her eyes filled with love and hope and tears of happiness. She knows they have a long road ahead of them, but she's ready to face it together with the two people she loves most in the world.)

(I slipped the ring on to her finger and got up and she hugs me and we kissed and Sue came running into our arms , We are going to be a family!!!) (He pulls Tina and Sue closer to him, his heart overflowing with happiness. He knows they've been through so much, but now he feels like anything is possible.)

"We're going to be a family, huh? That's the best thing I've ever heard." (He smiles, looking into Tina's eyes. He knows they have a long road ahead of them, but he feels more hopeful than he has in a long time.)

(She nods, her fingers playing with the ring on her finger. She can't believe this is really happening. She looks down at Sue, who is beaming with joy.)

"Yes, Sue. We're going to be a family." (She looks back up at Kenneth, her heart full of gratitude. She knows they've all been through so much, but now she feels like they're finally starting to heal.) (I look at Sue and she looked up at me and I held her tightly against me and said to her) From this day forward I have the pleasure of calling you my darling daughter

(tears was in my eyes as she looked at me)

(Her eyes widened in surprise, her cheeks flushing with warmth. She looks up at Kenneth, feeling a rush of love and pride. She leans into him, hugging him tightly.) "Thank you, Dad. I love you too." (She looks over at Tina, her eyes shining with happiness. She knows they've all been through so much, but now she feels like they're finally starting to move forward. She can't wait to see what the future holds for their new family.)

The End

Also by Kenneth Haines

A Tale of Escape

A group of Earthlings, including a young woman named Elara, is abducted by an invisible alien ship to become part of a cosmic exhibition. Facing the reality of being observed by an alien audience, they form a bond and ignite a longing for freedom. Together, they plot their escape, daring to dream of returning to their lives on Earth. As they navigate their captivity and fight for autonomy, they are tested but remain unbroken, driven by the hope of weaving their experiences back into humanity's story.

* * *

Whispers in the Sand

Amidst the whispers of the sand and the caress of the Autumn sea, a tale of survival unfolds on the shores of a forsaken island. Here, young Selene and her father carve out an existence, relying on the embrace of nature and each other. Their bond, once threatened by tragedy, burgeons under the trials they face in this barren refuge. But when the island yields an unexpected reunion, the fabric of their family is woven together once more, painting a poignant portrait of hope and resilience. In the cool embrace of a late afternoon's breeze, Selene's heart finds solace, and together, they etch a new beginning upon their souls—an indelible whisper in the fabric of time.

* * *

Tylorin

In the oppressive kingdom of Eldaf, where elves endure human cruelty, a desperate elf mother and her child find an unexpected ally in a compassionate human. Together, they embark on a perilous escape through secret paths and natural sanctuaries, aided by the whispers of the forest's denizens. Their journey leads them to an abandoned, tranquil cottage, where they begin a new life of resilience and love. United by courage and kinship, their bond transcends blood, offering hope and peace amidst the shadows of their past.

* * *

Echoes of Laughter, Echoes of Fear

In an abandoned amusement park reclaimed by nature, five young explorersâ€"three girls and two boysâ€"embark on an adventure filled with mystery and spectral intrigue. Amid peeling paint and rusting rides, they delve into the park's hidden sorrows, blending nostalgia with a sense of foreboding. As they confront both the park's secrets and their own fears, their journey becomes a test of courage, friendship, and the human spirit. In this eerie yet captivating odyssey, the line between joy and darkness blurs, leaving them to discover whether their bonds can light the way through the park's enigmatic shadows.

* * *

Sea of Shadows

Stranded on a solitary island, young Helene navigates a journey of survival and self-discovery, guided by the wisdom of her late father and the lessons of the untamed wilderness. Amid the island's deceptive tranquility, she transforms grief into resilience, building a sanctuary from remnants of the past and forging a future shaped by love and fortitude. Through hardship, Helene finds strength in enduring connections, her father's presence ever a guiding light. Her odyssey is one of emotional catharsis and renewal, where each dawn heralds the triumph of hope and the radiance of new beginnings.

* * *

Enchanted Citadel

In a realm where magic and technology intertwine, a group of elite space voyagers embarks on a perilous quest to recover the Chrono Crystal, an ancient gemstone vital for stabilizing the magical streams of their soaring sanctuary, the Enchanted Citadel. As they traverse vibrant yet conflicted planets, they face arcane guardians and looming threats of a malevolent siege. Amidst a cosmic battlefield where starships glide on waves of sorcery and science, the voyagers grapple with unity and betrayal, illuminating paths once hidden in the shadows.

* * *

Time has stopped

In *Time Has Stopped*, Elara and her band of weary travelers navigate an endless red desert, a harsh landscape that was once ruled by oceans and now conceals the secrets of a long-lost, water-bound civilization. Battling scorching heat, deceptive mirages, and unforgiving storms, their journey leads them to a colossal statue and an underground labyrinth echoing with the remnants of a forgotten world. Along the way, they form an unlikely bond with a mysterious creature whose loyalty may be their only hope for survival. As the desert tests their resilience and courage, each step comes with sacrifice, forcing them to confront how far they are willing to go to survive the relentless sands of time.

* * *

Starborn

In a distant cosmos, the crew of a valiant starship embarks on a perilous journey through the galactic veil, uncovering relics of the ancient Starborn civilizationâ€"artifacts of immense power and potential ruin. As they navigate celestial ruins and decipher esoteric transmissions, the explorers grapple with internal tensions and looming cosmic adversaries. Each discovery brings them closer to revolutionary breakthroughs while risking catastrophic consequences. Caught between enlightenment and oblivion, their odyssey becomes a profound reflection on the morality of progress and the price of knowledge, weaving a tale of human resolve amidst the vast, enigmatic expanse of the stars.

* * *

Tales of the Unknown

Word in the forest was that something wasn't right and the creatures were on edge and the slightest noise or movement made them run for cover. Word of this came to Sanction while he was foliage for food. A wagon rolled up and tossed a young girl child from it, she was wrapped inside a burlap potato bag and was tossed aside like trash. Child please dry them tears for you are safe in my forest, like I said no harm will come to you. She sits up and listens to his every word.

Jake found himself enjoying the solitude of the open road. That is, until his car started to sputter. A sudden jolt, leaving Jake stranded in the middle of nowhere. Desperate for help, Jake decided to head towards the building, hoping to find a phone or someone who could assist. Soon to find he has entered where time had stopped and the souls of who where left behind needed to be saved.

* * *

Whispers in the Sand

Amidst the whispers of the sand and the caress of the Autumn sea, a tale of survival unfolds on the shores of a forsaken island. Here, young Selene and her father carve out an existence, relying on the embrace of nature and each other. Their bond, once threatened by tragedy, burgeons under the trials they face in this barren refuge. But when the island yields an unexpected reunion, the fabric of their family is woven together once more, painting a poignant portrait of hope and resilience. In the cool embrace of a late afternoon's breeze, Selene's heart finds solace, and together, they etch a new beginning upon their souls—an indelible whisper in the fabric of time.

www.ingramcontent.com/pod-product-compliance
Lightning Source LLC
LaVergne TN
LVHW010500160826
845677LV00012B/2574

* 9 7 9 8 8 9 6 9 1 5 0 8 9 *